The THREE LITTLE PIGS

Count to 100

Grace Maccarone

pictures by
Pistacchio

Albert Whitman & Company
Chicago, Illinois

To Lois, Ralph, and Paul, of course!–GM

To my 2.0 wolf, Rude–NA

To my three little piggies,
Ingrid, Sofia, and Diana–JG

Library of Congress Cataloging-in-Publication
data is on file with the publisher.

Text copyright © 2015 by Grace Maccarone
Pictures copyright © 2015 by Albert Whitman & Company
Pictures by Pistacchio
Published in 2015 by Albert Whitman & Company
ISBN 978-0-8075-7901-5

Printed in China
10 9 8 7 6 5 4 3 2 1 HH 20 19 18 17 16 15

Design by Jordan Kost

For more information about Albert Whitman & Company,
visit our web site at www.albertwhitman.com.

Once upon a time, there was 1 mother pig.

She had **2** apples

but 3 sons.

She cut each of the apples in half to make **4** pieces.
And the **4** pigs shared them.

They were still quite hungry.

"It is time for you to seek your fortunes," the mother pig said to her sons.

And off they went.

The first little pig met a man with 5 bundles of straw. "Please, sir, give me that straw to build a house," said the first little pig.

The man did, and the first little pig built a house in the shape of a **cylinder**.

A wolf came along and knocked at the door. "Little pig, little pig, let me come in."

To which the pig answered, "No! Not by the hair of my chinny-chin-chin!"

This made the wolf angry and he said, "Then I'll huff and I'll puff and I'll blow your house in."

So he huffed and he puffed and he blew the house down.

Luckily, while the wolf was busy doing all that huffing and puffing, the first little pig had a chance to run away as fast as his little pig feet could carry him.

The second little pig met a boy with 6 big sticks and some sheets. "Please, sir, give me those sticks and sheets to build a house," said the second little pig.

The boy did, and the second little pig built a house in the shape of a **cone**.

Then the wolf came along and said, "Little pig, little pig, let me come in."

"No! Not by the hair of my chinny-chin-chin!"

"Then I'll huff and I'll puff and I'll blow your house in."

So the wolf huffed and he puffed and he blew the house down.

Luckily, while the wolf was busy doing all that huffing and puffing, the second little pig had a chance to run away as fast as his little pig feet could carry him.

The third little pig met a girl with 7 baskets of fluffy white wool.

"Would you like these 7 baskets of wool to build a house?" asked the girl.

The third little pig quickly declined. "No, thank you," he said. "Not wool."

Then the third little pig met a fellow with 8 bags of leaves.

"Would you like these 8 bags of leaves to build a house?" the fellow asked.

Once again, the third little pig quickly declined. "No, thank you," he said. "Not leaves."

A short while later, the third little pig met a woman with **9** boxes of rose petals.

"Would you like these **9** boxes of rose petals to build a house?" asked the woman.

The flower petals smelled very nice, but the third little pig declined once again. "Definitely not rose petals," he said. "No, thank you."

The third little pig continued on his way until he met a cat with 10 pails of peanuts.

"Would you like these 10 pails of peanuts to build a house?" asked the cat.

The third little pig, who liked peanuts very much, had to decline. He sighed, "No, thank you. Unfortunately, peanuts won't do."

Still thinking about fragrant flower petals and tasty peanuts, the third little pig walked along until he met a man with a load of bricks.

Bricks!

"Please, sir," said the third little pig. "Give me some bricks to build a house."

"How many?" asked the man.

The little pig gave this some thought.

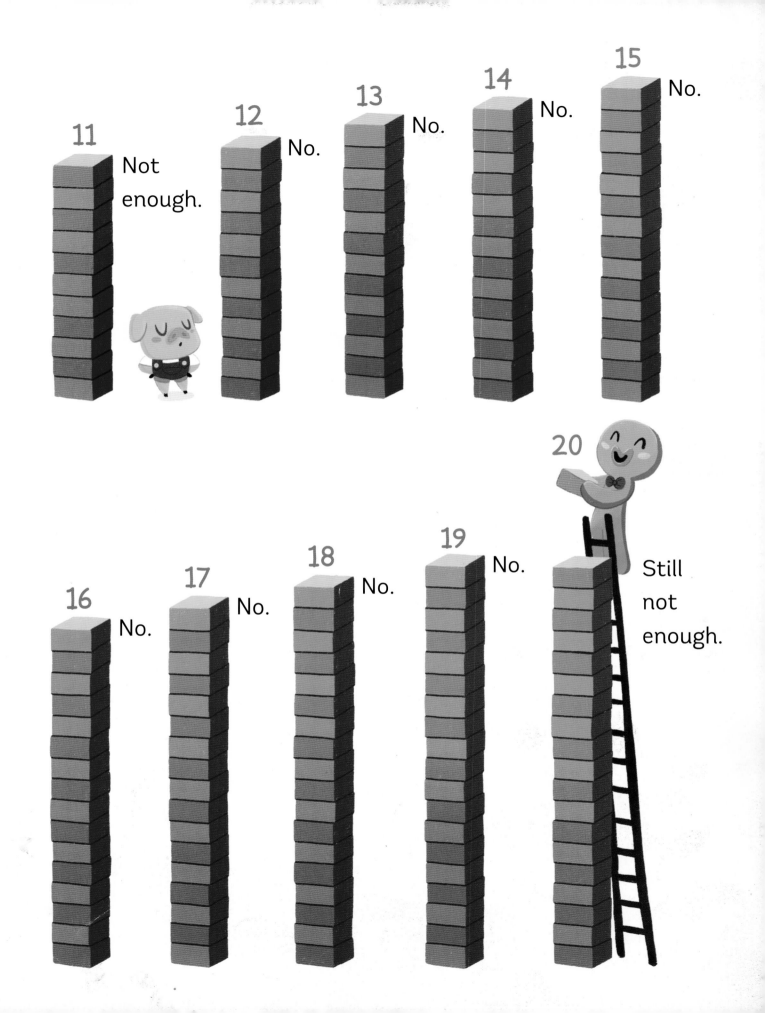

11 Not enough.

12 No.

13 No.

14 No.

15 No.

16 No.

17 No.

18 No.

19 No.

20 Still not enough.

"I need 100," the little pig said.

51	52	53	54	55
56	57	58	59	60

61	62	63	64	65
66	67	68	69	70

71	72	73	74	75
76	77	78	79	80

81	82	83	84	85
86	87	88	89	90

91	92	93	94	95
96	97	98	99	100

So with **100** bricks, the third little pig built his house in the shape of a **cube**.

Then the wolf came, as he did to the other little pigs, and said, "Little pig, little pig, let me come in."

"No! Not by the hair on my chinny-chin-chin!"

"Then I'll huff and I'll puff and I'll blow your house in."

Well, he huffed and he puffed and he huffed and puffed and he puffed and huffed, but he could not blow the house down.

The wolf was so tired and hungry
he decided to become a vegetarian.

The third little pig had a lovely supper too!
And he and his family lived happily ever after.

This is the
first little pig.

This is the
second little pig.

And this is the
third little pig.

1st. That's me!

2nd. That's me!

3rd. That's me!

My house is
a cylinder.

My house is
a cone.

My house is
a cube.

2 is one more than 1.
3 is one more than 2.
4 is one more than 3.

I want 2 apples.

I want 3 apples.

I want 4 apples.

Count to 100 by ones.

Count to 100 by tens.

1	2	3	4	5	6	7	8	9	10
11	12	13	14	15	16	17	18	19	20
21	22	23	24	25	26	27	28	29	30
31	32	33	34	35	36	37	38	39	40
41	42	43	44	45	46	47	48	49	50
51	52	53	54	55	56	57	58	59	60
61	62	63	64	65	66	67	68	69	70
71	72	73	74	75	76	77	78	79	80
81	82	83	84	85	86	87	88	89	90
91	92	93	94	95	96	97	98	99	100